THIS WALKER BOOK BELONGS TO:

_____

_____

_____

_____

For Helen with love
S.H.

For Christle, Mimi, Ruth and Didi
H.C.

First published 1986 by
Walker Books Ltd
87 Vauxhall Walk
London SE11 5HJ

This edition published 1988

14 15 13

Text © 1986 Sarah Hayes
Illustrations © 1986 Helen Craig

Printed in Hong Kong

British Library Cataloguing in Publication Data
A catalogue record for this book is
available from the British Library.

ISBN 0-7445-1304-9

THIS IS THE
BEAR
AND THE
PICNIC LUNCH

WRITTEN BY

Sarah Hayes

ILLUSTRATED BY

Helen Craig

WALKER BOOKS
AND SUBSIDIARIES
LONDON · BOSTON · SYDNEY

This is the boy
who packed a lunch

of sandwiches, crisps and
an apple to crunch.

This is the bear
who guarded the box

while the boy went to find
his shoes and socks.

This is the dog
who sneaked past the chair

towards the lunch and
the brave guard bear.

This is the bear
with his eyes half closed
who did not notice
the dog's black nose.

This is the bear
who was sound asleep

when the dog performed
a tremendous leap…

on to the table…

down to the floor…

and off to hide

behind the door . . .

and all that he left
of the picnic lunch
was an empty box and
the apple to crunch.

This is the boy
who looked everywhere

for his lunch and his dog
and his brave guard bear.

This is the boy
who heard the munch

of a dog and a bear
eating picnic lunch.

This is the boy
who tried to be angry

but found he was
suddenly terribly hungry.

This is the boy
who packed a new lunch
of sandwiches, crisps and
the apple to crunch.
And this is the bear who said,
"Haven't you guessed?
Indoor picnics are the best!"